FRIENDS
OF ACPL

Harry's Got a Girlfriend!

Harry's Got a Girlfriend!

By Ulli Schubert

Illustrated by Wolfgang Slawski

Translated by J. Alison James

SCHOLASTIC INC.

New York Toronto London Auckland Sydney
Mexico City New Delhi Hong Kong

For my niece, Annika, in Boston – U.S.

ISBN 0-439-10131-X

Copyright © 1999 by Nord-Süd Verlag AG, Gossau Zürich,
Switzerland. First published in Switzerland under the title
Hannes geht zum Mädchen-Geburstag!
English translation copyright © 1999 by North-South Books Inc.
All rights reserved. Published by Scholastic Inc.,
555 Broadway, New York, NY 10012,
by arrangement with North-South Books Inc.
SCHOLASTIC and associated logos are trademarks
and/or registered trademarks of Scholastic Inc.

12 11 10 9 8 7 6 5 4 3 2 1   0 1 2 3 4 5/0

Printed in the U.S.A.   23

First Scholastic printing, January 2000

Contents

After the Game

Harry was in the locker room with his best
friends. "Where is my school bag?" he asked.
"Hey, Tony, did you see my bag?"

"Here it is!" said George, grinning.

"Give it here!" Harry grabbed for the bag. But George quickly tossed it over to Steve. Harry tackled George and held him in a headlock.

"Cut it out!" squealed George.

"Let him go!" cried Steve.

"First give me my bag!" Harry squeezed tighter.

"Come and get it!" Steve ran outside.

Harry ran after him. But he stopped at the door, laughing. "Thanks for carrying my bag for me," he called.

Steve stopped short. Then he tossed the school bag to Harry. "You win," he said.

Harry, Steve, George, and Tony went down the path to the bus stop.

"That was a great game!" said George. "Dodgeball is so much fun! The girls' team didn't stand a chance against us!"

"Did you see how I got Tanya out?" Steve demonstrated: "Right . . . left . . . fire!" He slapped his thigh.

"I really got Michelle," said Harry. "She thinks she's so good at dodging."

"Yeah, that was great," said George. "She was really upset!"

"We showed them who the champs are," Harry said.

"Yeah," said Tony. "They won't challenge the boys to another game soon."

The Invitation

The four boys slapped high fives.
Suddenly Tony hissed, "Watch out!"
Five girls grinned at them from across
the street.

"Why are they so happy?" Harry asked.
"They lost!"

"Why are they staring at us like that?"
Tony asked.

"Let's get out of here," said George.

"Are you nuts?" Tony was indignant. "I
don't run away from girls."

"But there are five of them," said Steve.
"And Tanya knows judo. Come on. Let's go."

"Too late." Tony pointed to the street. "They're coming over."

The girls crossed the street and planted themselves in front of the boys.

Michelle looked at Harry.

Harry flinched. For a moment, he thought that she was still angry and was going to punch him. But then he saw the envelope.

"Here. For you," she said.

Harry hesitated, then took it.

Michelle turned and disappeared into the group of girls. They walked away giggling.

Harry stared at the envelope.

"What's inside?" asked Tony.

"I don't know." Harry said.

"Open it up!" insisted Steve.

Harry tore open the envelope and took out a piece of paper. There was a picture on it. A golden sun shone in a blue sky over a green meadow. A table was set up with chairs, and

there was something square with smoke
pouring out of it.

Harry had no idea what it was supposed to
be. A picture? he thought. Why would
Michelle give him a picture?

"There's writing on the back," said Steve, starting to read in a girly voice:

"Dear Harry, I would like to ..."

"Cut it out!" Harry said. He tried to fold up the letter. But Steve was faster. He grabbed it from Harry's hands and climbed up on the school wall.

Harry leapt for Steve's feet.

"Give it back!" he cried "It's mine!" He tried to climb the wall.

But George and Tony held him back. Harry stomped and shouted, but he had no chance against the two of them.

Steve called for attention: "Hey, listen to this!"

"*Dear Harry, I would like to invite you to my birthday party....*"

"A girl's birthday party!" squealed George and Tony.

"I said give it back!" growled Harry. He twisted and turned, but he couldn't get free.

"Harry's got a girlfriend!" teased Tony.

"You're crazy!" Harry tugged, turned, and finally broke free. He jumped up, grabbed the letter, and ran away.

"Harry's got a girlfriend! Harry's got a girlfriend!" sang Steve, Tony, and George.

Michelle

Harry ran and ran. For a long time he still heard laughter. At last he turned the corner. Harry ran up to his building. He rang and rang on the doorbell until his mother pushed the buzzer. Then he raced up the stairs.

"Why are you running so fast?" asked his mother. "Is someone chasing you?"

Harry threw himself into her arms. "They are so mean!" he sobbed.

"Who is so mean?" asked his mother. "What happened?"

"Michelle invited me. But I can't go to a girl's birthday party!"

Harry rubbed the tears from his eyes and ran to his room.

He flung his school bag in the corner near his desk. Then he crawled into the cave that he'd made a few days ago. Harry smoothed out the crumpled letter and read it carefully. There wasn't much there that Steve hadn't already told the whole world, other than that Michelle was turning eight, and her party was tomorrow.

Harry turned the letter around and looked at the picture that Michelle had drawn. Suddenly Harry smiled. For a minute, he was glad that Michelle had invited him. But then he remembered how the other boys had laughed at him. They knew how much Harry hated girls.

All girls. Except maybe Michelle. At least she wasn't as silly as the rest, he thought. Sometimes she was even nice. Like when she brought her rabbit to school and let him hold it for a long time. Or when she turned around during science lessons and whispered the answers to him.

Or when she shared her snack with him.
Harry smiled at the thought.

Actually there were quite a lot of times
when Harry really did like her.

The Shopping Trip

Harry's mother called him to dinner. He crawled out of his cave, washed his hands, and went into the kitchen. His father was there, too. On Fridays he always came home early from the office.

Harry jumped on his father's back. "What are we doing tonight, Dad?"

"Shopping," said his father. He grabbed Harry and swung him around. "Just the two of us. We're going right after dinner."

"Great!" cried Harry.

"I knew this would be the first place you'd go," his father said when Harry headed straight for the toy store. He laughed. "Oh well, we can go in."

It was a huge toy store.

Harry checked out an intergalactic warrior robot, tested a new video game, and watched two boys throwing giant dice.

"Are you looking for something in particular?" asked his father.

"No," Harry said. He stared longingly at the enormous racetrack that was set up in the middle of the store.

A bunch of kids were waiting to race.
Harry really wanted to try it.

"No, Harry," said his father. "It would take
all night just waiting for your turn."

Suddenly Harry saw his friends, and they saw him.

"Look!" said Steve. "There's Harry."

"He's come to buy a present," said Tony loudly. "A *girl's* present."

"Yes," said George, grinning. "Harry is going to a *girl's* birthday party!"

The three of them stood at a safe distance and laughed at him. Harry wanted to ram them into the floor.

"Come on," his father said. He laid his hand on Harry's shoulder and they just walked past Steve, Tony, and George.

In the supermarket, Harry and his father bought groceries. Then they picked up two videos. And then they got ice-cream cones. The whole time Harry's father didn't say a word about the birthday party.

A Birthday Present

Harry's father didn't mention it until later when he came to say good night. "What was all that about?" he asked.

Harry told him about the invitation. "But I'll never go," he said.

"Why not?"

Harry just shook his head.

"Because Michelle is a girl?"

Harry nodded. "I just can't go," he said. "I'd never hear the end of it. Besides, I don't know how to play with girls."

"You played with girls in preschool," his father said. "And I remember you had a lot of fun."

"But that was different," Harry said. "Nobody said anything about it. Everyone played together. Now if I think a girl is nice, the boys laugh at me."

"But Michelle is your friend," said his father. "Would you stop being friends with someone just because someone else didn't approve?" He smiled proudly at his son. "I know you better than that. But what I'm surprised at is that those boys weren't invited, too. Maybe they're just jealous that you're going and they aren't."

Harry rolled onto his side and snuggled under the covers.

"You know what?" said his father. "You can go to the party, and if you don't like it you can just leave."

Harry thought about that. It was a good idea. "How would I leave?" he asked.

"Tell them it's been a lovely party, but you've got to go. Then call me, and I'll come right away to get you."

"You mean it?"

"I promise." His father tucked Harry in. "Now go to sleep. Good night."

"Good night, Dad."

Harry was asleep before his father closed the door.

The next morning, Harry leaped out of bed. He needed a present to bring to the party. And he'd dreamed up the perfect idea: a big paper cone full of surprises!

Right after breakfast, he went to work. He decorated thick paper and rolled it up into a big cone, then sealed it tight with glue and tape. Then he packed the cone full of lots of tiny presents: a magic card game, a glow-in-the-dark pencil sharpener, a mini puzzle, a couple of markers, and a handful of marbles.

Harry showed his mother his present.

"What a good idea!" she said.

She got out a bag of chocolates and put it on top. "There," she said. "Now it's perfect." Together they glued tissue paper inside the top of the cone. Then they tied a big bow around it. The birthday surprise was finished!

At the Party

Finally it was time to go to the party.
Harry's father drove him to Michelle's.
"Have fun!" he said.

Harry got out, reached in the window, and
grabbed his father's arm. "You promise you'll
come and get me if I call?"

"Of course," said his father. So Harry let
go of his arm and went to the door.

"Oh, Harry!" said Michelle's mother. "I have to apologize. Michelle's cousins, twin boys, were supposed to come, but they got sick. I told Michelle she had to invite at least one boy to keep them company. So now you're here on your own. I hope it's all right."

Harry nodded, surprised.

Michelle's garden looked exactly like the picture she'd drawn. There was a big table in the middle of the lawn.

Around it sat five girls: Tanya, Nancy, Christine, Julia, and, of course, Michelle. They stared at him.

Harry gave Michelle his present.

"Thank you," said Michelle, and she opened it right away. "Hey, wow!" she said.

Harry smiled, embarrassed.

First there was hot chocolate and birthday cake. Exactly like at a boy's birthday party, Harry thought.

The girls chatted cheerfully. Harry didn't feel comfortable. He didn't understand anything they were talking about. Manicures and pedicures and this doll whose hair turned blue when you brushed it with water. It was as if they were in their own universe, orbiting around him. He tried to look interested, and wondered to himself how long he had to wait before it was polite to phone his father to come and get him.

But then Michelle's father came out and took them into the back field to fly a kite. Everyone got a turn to hold the line. The wind was so strong that the kite flew really high and even did tricks.

Then they played "I Spy" and badminton. Afterwards, they went into the basement, where Michelle's father had built her a race-track just like the one in the toy store. Everyone got lots of turns to race the two electric cars.

Suddenly Harry smelled smoke.

"Something's on fire!" he said, alarmed.

"Oh, that's good news," said Michelle's father. "That means we can eat soon." They went back outside. The grill was smoking and spitting, and the table was already set.

There were hot dogs, hamburgers, potato salad, chocolate pudding, and juice.

Harry ate until he couldn't eat another bite.

"You kids have enough time for one more game," Michelle's mother announced.

"What shall we play?" asked Tanya.

"'Blindman's Bluff!'" suggested Julia.

Michelle got to be "It" first, since it was her birthday. She stuck out her arms and groped for someone. Then suddenly she spun around and grabbed. It was Tanya, but Michelle didn't know that. She had to try to find out who it was by asking yes-or-no questions.

"Are you a girl?" she asked.

"Yes!" squeaked Tanya, in a fake voice. Harry giggled.

"Do you have blond hair?"

"No," growled Tanya.

"Do you like grapes but not raisins?"

"Yes," said Tanya, laughing

Michelle shouted, "It's Tanya!"

Almost everyone got to be "It." But Harry escaped each time. He was glad, since he didn't know the little details that would have helped him guess who he'd grabbed. He learned a lot about the girls who were there. And they *all* seemed nice, not just Michelle.

A Big Surprise

Finally it was time to go. Parents were coming and ringing the doorbell. As the kids left, they each thanked Michelle for inviting them.

Harry wanted so much to tell Michelle what a great time he'd had. But he felt too shy. When he thought of all the things he'd been worried about, and of all the things his friends had said, he got embarrassed. This party had been nothing like he'd expected.

"Harry!" called Michelle's mother. "Your father is here to pick you up!"

"Bye, Michelle," Harry said. "I've got to go. Thank you for asking me to your party. It was a lot of fun." He smiled shyly.

"Thanks for coming, Harry!" Michelle said, and she threw her arms around his neck and gave him a kiss on the cheek.

Harry turned red. But Michelle didn't seem to notice. "I'm glad you had a good time," she said. "You're so much nicer than my cousins!"

Harry felt a little dizzy. It was over, and he'd had a lot of fun. And Michelle thought he was nice.

Harry's father was waiting at the door. "How was it?" he asked.

"It was great," Harry said.

"Well, I have a surprise for you," his father said.

In the backseat of the car sat Tony, George and Steve!

"They asked if they could come along to pick you up," said Harry's father.

"Hi," said George.

"What happened?" asked Tony.

"Give us all the details," said Steve.

Harry swung in beside them. "Let's start with the food," he said. The boys were drooling by the time he had finished telling them the menu.

"And best of all," Harry said, "she's got a huge racetrack. I got seven turns!"

The boys groaned. "You're so lucky!"

"If she asks you back to her house, could you see if we can come, too?" asked George.

"Okay, but no girl jokes," said Harry.

"Are you kidding?" said Tony. "With kites, a racetrack, and great food—this is serious!"

Harry nodded and smiled. It was great to have friends!

About the Author

Ulli Schubert was born in Hamburg,
Germany. After school, he worked at a vari-
ety of jobs: construction worker, forklift
operator, tea packer at the docks, sleeping-
car attendant, sports reporter, truck driver,
and waiter. In 1984, after studying to become
a teacher, he started to write—first he
worked as a children's book critic, then he
began writing his own books.

Ulli Schubert still lives in Hamburg. This
is his first book for North-South.

About the Illustrator

Wolfgang Slawski was born in Neumünster, Germany. He spent his early years in Hamburg. After studying at Hamburg's Technical School of Design, focusing on illustration, Wolfgang Slawski joined with other illustrators to form the group "Atelier 9." Since then he has worked as a freelance graphic artist. He is the author and illustrator of two picture books published by North-South, *Captain Jonathan Sails the Sea* and *The Friendship Trip*.